MW00952471

Black girl Magic

This book belongs to:

Copyright © 2022
Aaliyah Wilson

All rights reserved.
No parts of this publication may be reproduced, distributed, or transmitted in any form, or by any means,
including photocopying, recording or other electronic or mechanical methods, without prior written
permission from the publisher.

ALL about ME!

by...................

My favorite color is...

This is me!

My favorite food is...

I'm .... years old.

My favorite animal is...

My favorite movie is...

In each heart write something positive about yourself...

Mirror, mirror on the wall....who's the kindest child of all?
Write or draw as many things as you can that you love
about yourself. For example, you can write I love my curly
hair, or I love my brown eyes.

Connect the numbers

Maze 1

How to draw a unicorn

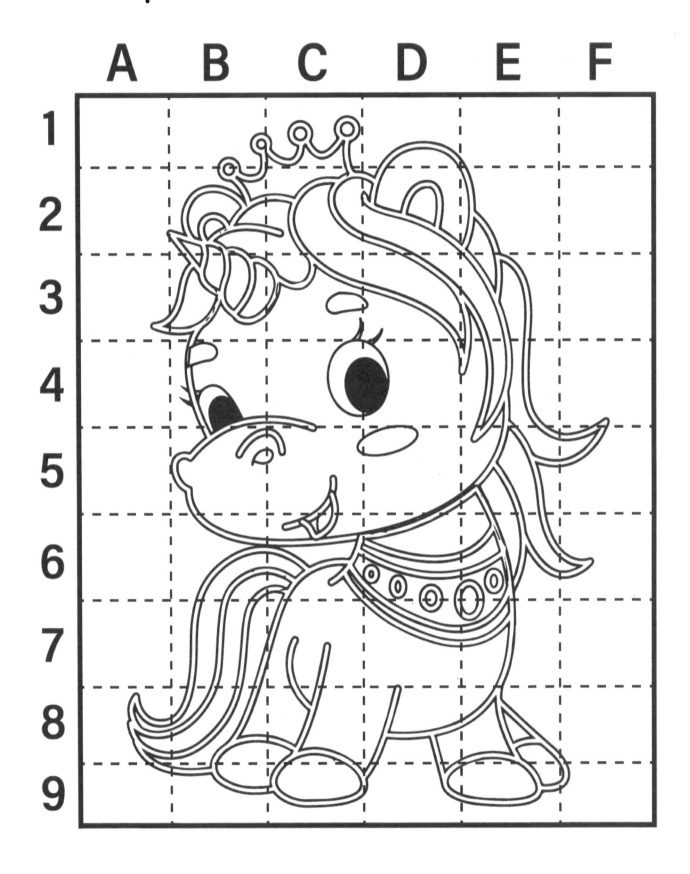

Your turn!

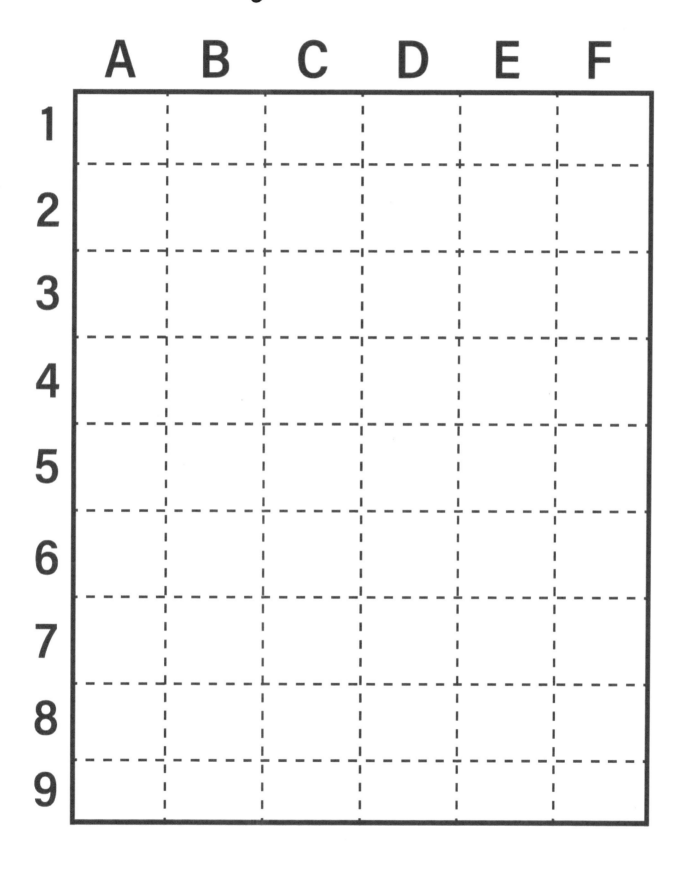

Connect the numbers

Color and cut

Connect the numbers

Maze 2

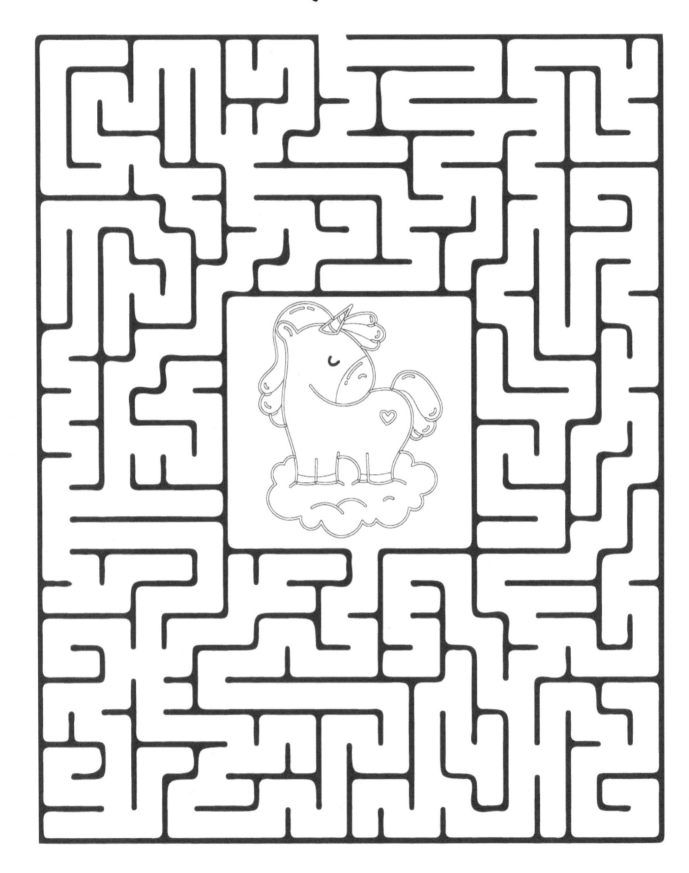

Color and cut

Connect the numbers

Maze 3

Connect the numbers

Solutions

Hi there,

If you enjoyed this coloring book please don't forget to leave a review on Amazon.

Just a simple review will help me a lot.

Thank you,

Aaliyah Wilson

♡

Made in United States
Troutdale, OR
12/17/2024

26765708R00040